THE SISTERS

"Something Is Sinister At That Place"

JAMES ROBERTS

Edited by
JAMES ROBERTS
Illustrated by
JAMES ROBERTS

Cover Design Copyright © 2020 James Roberts

Cover Art Copyright © 2020 James Roberts

Illustrations Copyright © 2020 James Roberts

ISBN: 978-1-7361234-4-7

Library of Congress Control Number: 2020923097

Published by James Roberts Publishing

Printed in the United States Of America

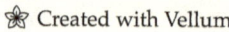 Created with Vellum

CONTENTS

INTRODUCTION

This book is a work of fiction and continues alongside the Julia Lillus Series of Crime Thrillers by James Roberts.

"Let me say that I really was not looking for something from her, but if the invitation was put in front of me, I would be tempted to take her up on it. I, being a man of early forties, would be quite delighted to be taken in with such a raven beauty as she."

Chapter One

ARRIVING AT THE RESORT

*I*t is a cold day in February when traveling to the Pocono Mountains to meet some friends at a resort. It is late, around 10:00 PM, and I still have to travel fifty more miles to my destination.

When I finally arrive at the resort, it is well after midnight, and as I approach the entrance and ring the doorbell, a middle-aged woman greets me at the door with a smile that has the appearance of sleeplessness. I apologize for my late arrival when she hands me the key to my cabin located in the woods.

I must regress a little and describe the resort and its surroundings. The resort is well known for its programs centered on living in peace with the environment. All the accommodations, including the resort itself, is nestled in a dense grove of pines in a valley with mountains on either side. There are trails throughout the wooded area, and peacefulness is felt with the occasional sound of a hoot owl marking its territory.

My cabin is located about halfway up the gentle slope to the higher ground leading to the mountains. I slip the key into the entrance lock and immediately greeted with a warm glow of embers in the fireplace. I didn't take the time to locate the friends I was to meet; the hour was now past 1:00 AM.

I quickly head to the shower and then make way to the bed, which has a huge duck down spread with which to envelope me in pure warmth.

Morning arrives with the crow of a nearby rooster. I open one eye to see the glaring daylight shimmering through the cabin window over my bed. I then draw the duck down spread over my head to get more sleep before I have to get up.

As you might have guessed, it wasn't only a few minutes later, and the breakfast bell is being rung. I knew from past experiences at resorts if one did not get to the Center Hall for breakfast when the bell is rung, you have a slight chance of getting anything to eat.

I enter the Center Hall only to find a handful of guests, but no one there is the friends I was supposed to meet. As a matter of fact, all the guests are women.

There, on the table, is a guest book that everyone would have signed upon arrival. Since I arrived so late, I entered my name immediately before I sat down in the lounge chair.

Bacon, eggs, sausage, fruit, and some kind of rolls and a type of cake was served. I rise from my lounge and pile as much on my plate as I can fit. I am not a lunch kind of guy, so this breakfast has to last me until dinner time.

As I sit down again in the lounge chair, I once again look for my friends, although I do not see their names in the register. Maybe they arrived late as well and just decided to forgo breakfast.

Chapter Two

AMANDA

*S*uddenly out of the kitchen door comes a girl with the beverages for the morning. I fix my eyes on her due to her uncanny beauty. I would guess she is at the age of thirty, no more than thirty-two. She is tall and slender with long jet black hair. Her skin tone is that of Asian-type glow, but she is not of Asian culture. Her eyebrows are as dark as her hair, and she has slight dimples in her cheeks with a soft but chiseled face. She is wearing Yoga Pants™, which give way to her well-toned torso and legs.

I have a thing about women and their build around the crotch area. There are women with no space in the crotch area, just inner thigh to inner thigh. Then some have varying space between their thighs. This girl has quite a space in her crotch area, yet her hips are not overly broad. Due to this physical attribute, she has quite the swagger when she walks.

Her breasts are not overly large, but they are ample enough to matter as she walks past me wearing a tank type top. They are firm enough not to need the support of a brazier, and their bounce is subtle.

As I sit in my lounger, I keep an eye on her watching her move as she walks towards me and passes me on the way to serving the other guests. It is my turn for her to offer a breakfast drink. She asks me what drink I would like, in a most pleasant tone of voice; I opt for the tomato juice. As she bends towards me to give me my drink, I get a better glimpse of her breasts, and what I had thought about them was grossly underestimated. They are firmer than I thought with no downward sag as she bends down towards me. Her nipples, not quite erect, are large and inviting.

After the encounter, she retreats to the kitchen, and I don't see her for the rest of the morning.

It is mid-afternoon, and I realize that my friends hadn't made it to the resort, so I am by myself with the festivities. At noon there is a hike planned through the wooded area. A resort faculty member is leading the way as we follow. Usually, it is one of the fitness guys or ladies as the guide, but today is different. As some of the guests and I walk out to the start of the trail, I quickly notice that the girl from the kitchen, the one I had been admiring at breakfast, is to be the guide this afternoon. My reaction is most surprising and unexpected, but I guess the breakfast endeavor heightened my response. I immediately turn from facing her, hoping that she doesn't see the sudden bulge in my pants and wait impatiently for it to resolve itself to normalcy. I guess she has gotten to me.

Halfway up the trail, the guests are starting to broaden their distance from one another to the point of me being pretty much alone. All of a sudden, behind me, I hear the familiar tone of voice as she asks me my name. I turn to face the raven beauty and sheepishly answer with my name. "My name is Louis LaMont, but you can call me Louie." She tells me that her name is Amanda, and she is newly hired for teaching gymnastics and meditation. She also tells me that she is a massage therapist. As she talks to me, I can't stop staring at her mouth. It is as if she is inviting me to something, as she deliberately positions her tongue between her lips as she speaks, moistening her dark lips. Being up close now, I can see that her eye color matches her hair color, but they are beautiful with a glimpse of green-blue. She is wearing a long winter-type coat, so I am not able to see her whole body up close, but in walking with her up the trail as we talk, I can tell she is hiding something special under the coat.

Let me say that I really am not looking for something from her, but if the invitation is put in front of me, I will be tempted to take her up on it. I, being a man of early forties, will be quite delighted to be taken in with such a raven beauty as she.

Just before we catch up with the rest of the guests, she offers me a free massage later in the evening. I do not know what to say to her. Of course, I want the massage, but where would it lead? Nothing I hope... or maybe...

I oblige and ask what time she wants me to show up. She tells me shortly after dinner to meet her in the Center Hall, and she will lead me to where I will get the massage.

Chapter Three

THE MASSAGE

*A*fter we part from the trail walk, I walk to my cabin to rest. I can't help thinking about Amanda and kind of wish that she had not given me the opportunity for a free massage. How will I act? I have had massages before but not by a female. What do I do when she reaches areas that will give rise?

Maybe I should just tell her that I won't be able to make it. Perhaps I can say to her that I am not feeling well. No, I can't do that to her. I believe she has drawn me in, and I have no escape.

Amanda is not serving dinner this evening, but I catch a glimpse of her leaving the kitchen. She glances over to me while I am sitting in my lounger and gives me an inviting smile with parsed lips and a tongue waving me in.

Dinner is over, and I retreat to my cabin, again wondering what I may be getting myself into. If she makes advances towards me, should I ignore them or oblige? Oh, what is it I am thinking? She is just nice to me, a guest, and I am reading way too much into it. What if I am? Would it hurt me to be seduced, or maybe I want to be seduced?

I enter the Center Hall, and Amanda is sitting in the lounger I claim as my own while I am here at the resort. She is wearing sweat pants, and a very loose halter top with a low cut V-neck laced together with a cloth tie. As I get closer to her, I can smell a beautiful scent that is mesmerizing, and it gets stronger as she rises from the lounger and whisks by me. I believe she has purposely applied it between her breasts.

I follow her up the steps leading to the second floor, all the time watching her ass sway back and forth as if it, too, is inviting me. As we reach the room where I am to get the massage, Amanda shows me where I can undress and says that she will be back in a few minutes. I strip down to my underwear and immediately lie face down on the massage table, contemplating whether I should remove my shorts. To get the best out of the massage, I should be completely nude, and in that this massage is free, I must endure as much relaxation as I can. I immediately stand up and remove my undershorts. I think about possible consequences if Amanda comes back; I get under the covers quickly.

Upon Amanda's return, she turns on some relaxing music and dims the lights. She asks me how deep of a massage I want, and I tell her she can press reasonably deep with the Swedish Style Massage she is about to give me. I nestle my face into the face cushion as she pulls the covers down to my waste and starts the massage. She is excellent at what she does. I have had other massages that were not half as good as what she is demonstrating.

I am so relaxed that I almost fall asleep when she asks me to turn over. As I lie there, she slowly starts working my legs. I feel her hands slip between my inner thighs near my torso. I immediately and involuntarily react, and my penis starts to rise as it becomes engorged with blood. She stops at that point and moves toward my head. As she turns, I notice that the ties of her halter top have become undone. She reaches over my head and places her hands on my waist, and her breasts clearly show themselves to me as they fall forward out of her top. I try not to look, but one of them is inches from my face. The nipples I witnessed earlier in the day are now fully erect. Her areola, large as half dollars, are crimson. She moves more toward my head to place her hands lower on my waist, and suddenly one of her nipples is almost touching my lips.

I don't know exactly what I am thinking, but at a moment's notice, I latch onto the nipple with my lips and start sucking. Amanda then lowers herself so that her breast lies against my face. I raise my hands and immediately push her breasts from me. I sheepishly tell her that I am sorry and I don't know why I did that to her. She tells me not to worry, for it is mostly her fault not noticing that the ties on her halter had come undone. However, I swore to myself she untied them when she had her back to me.

She finishes the massage without any other incidents. I thank her for the great job she did. She tells me that I can have another free massage anytime I want it.

Chapter Four

THE DREAM

After leaving Amanda, I go back to my cabin to think. At first, I am quite embarrassed that I had suckled her breast, but then I realize that deep down, it was the time of my life, and I liked it very much. I feel like masturbating thinking about the incident, but I think better of it. I don't know why, or do I?

After some time enjoying the fire in the fireplace, I am succumbing to sleep. I strip off my clothes and nestle myself under the duck down cover. I lie thinking about Amanda, her breast, and me sucking her nipple, until I fall into a deep sleep.

I dream more about Amanda, and suddenly my cock is aroused, but not that is unusual because it becomes erect at times during my sleep anyway. I feel a little cold probably because the fire has died down. I dream that I go further than just suckling Amanda's breast. I believe I am dreaming I have entered her. My cock feels like it has found a home in her vagina. I feel the in and out motions, and my hips are moving in concert with it. There is a certain amount of wetness I feel on my cock. I also feel warmth as if I am fucking her on my back, and she is lying on top of me as she thrusts herself onto my cock. Boy, it sure feels good! Then suddenly, I feel the release as I ejaculate. How can that be? I am dreaming, aren't I?

Morning comes, and I find myself uncovered. Boy, what a crazy dream. I start to get up to go to the bathroom when I notice a small release of semen coming from my cock. On further inspection, I see that I must have ejaculated in my dream just like I thought. There is semen all over the down cover, and my thighs are damp with sweat. I never had a 'wet dream' as they call it, but it sure was a fun ride. The funny thing is, my groin smells like the familiar aroma of pussy. How the hell can that be?

It is a good thing I hadn't masturbated earlier because I might not have experienced fucking Amanda in my dream.

The breakfast bell rings just as I am getting out of the shower. I quickly get dressed and rush over to the Center Hall.

I settle myself down in my lounger just as Amanda comes walking over to me. She asks me if I had a restful sleep. I don't dare tell her that I dreamt fucking her. I tell her my sleep was very relaxing and asks her what is in store for today. She says she is leading a Yoga Class and that she wants me to attend. I tell her that I am not really into Yoga, but because she invited me, I will go to class. After thinking about it, I will be able to view her in some pretty interesting, if not provocative moves. I don't think I should start thinking about her like that, but that dream last night made it a little more intimate for me.

The yoga class is exciting. I see her ass in very provocative positions and notice, once again, the gap she has between her thighs at her crotch—no problem getting between her legs and entering her cherry. Oh, hell, I need to stop thinking like this. I must admit her bare midriff is enticing giving way to her navel. I wouldn't mind sticking my tongue into it. It turns me on thinking about it.

After class, Amanda invites me to another free massage tomorrow evening. I accept only with the promise to her that I will not touch her. She assures me she will make sure she won't tempt me. I kind of wish she hadn't said that because I am starting to like her in a very intimate way.

After dinner, I once again retreat to my cabin to unwind, and yet it doesn't take too long before I am sleepy again. It is kind of unusual because I am a 'night owl' type person. As soon as my head hits the pillow, I am fast asleep.

Another dream overcomes me after I start thinking about Amanda and suckling her breast. I can see her. She is standing next to me while I am lying in my bed. I look up at her, and she is bare-chested, and her breasts are full looking, with her nipples very erect like they were over me while on the massage table. She bends down to center one of her breasts on my lips. I gently take her nipple in my mouth and start sucking. She then gently pulls away from me as her nipple slips out of my lips. Immediately she directs the other breast to my lips as I then suckle her other nipple. She starts to rotate between her breasts so that first, I am sucking one, and then I am sucking the other. She pulls away from me, and I suddenly feel my cock stiffening, and the warmth, again, is felt and a wet feeling along with an up and down motion on my shaft. The movement continues, and an eruption of semen is had.

When morning comes, I awaken and begin thinking about my dream with Amanda. Again, I had another 'wet dream', and I am concerned the cleaning staff will notice the dried semen on the bed cover.

At breakfast, I get an inviting smile from Amanda. She comes over to me while I am sitting in my lounger before she serves any of the other guests. I ask her how often the cleaning staff comes to change the bedding. She tells me that today is the day, but she will replace them for me. I thank her but tell her it is not necessary. She pats me on the cheek and tells me it is no problem. Before she leaves, she reminds me of the massage later this evening.

Chapter Five

A MORE INTENSE MASSAGE

By the time my massage appointment comes, I have had an entire day to think about Amanda and my dreams about her. I decide if she makes a move on me, I will reciprocate.

I quickly get under the covers of the massage table as Amanda enters the room. Her attire is the same as it was with the other massage. Everything starts the same, and I notice she has put more of that sweet perfume on her. This time it smells all over her body and not just between her breasts.

By the time she gets to my legs, I am feeling very sleepy, much like every evening after dinner. She places her hands against my inner thighs and massages the erroneous areas with a gentle kneading motion. My cock immediately responds to her advances. Just as I see it rise above my legs, I fall into a deep sleep. I start to dream again, and this time I feel a weight upon my body, and I smell Amanda's perfume. It is powerful. I try to open my eyes, but they will not open. I am not sure what I feel down at my groin, but for some reason, I feel a wet and warm feeling come over my face. I get the urge to open my mouth and stick out my tongue. Then all of a sudden, someone is kissing me. I feel the lips on my lips, and they are very wet and warm. I assume that it must be Amanda kissing me. She has her lips parted, and I stick my tongue in her mouth to feel her tongue.

As I am coming out of my dream and my sleep, I notice Amanda sitting in her chair next to the massage table and asks me if I had a relaxing sleep. I apologize to her for falling asleep during the massage, and she tells me not to worry, and it sometimes happens. As I start to get up to put on my clothes, still under the covers, I notice I had another 'wet dream'. Amanda sees the astonishment on my face and asks me what is the matter. I turn all red and sheepishly tell her I had some sort of accident and soiled her sheet. She tells me that it sometimes happens and not to worry about it. She leaves the room so I can get dressed. When Amanda returns, she says to me I am good for another free massage before I leave the resort.

I look her in the eyes and ask her if she is sure about that. I tell her she is not making any money off of me. She smiles and places her hand on my shoulder as she tells me it is her pleasure.

Just then, I think I notice wetness on her halter top, but just pass it off as sweat due to the fact giving a massage is grueling work.

Chapter Six

THE REVELATION

*A*nother dinner, followed by another sleepy evening. The dream with Amanda continues, and another "wet dream" follows. By this time, I am sure I am being seduced in my sleep, and it is with Amanda.

Breakfast comes, and I cannot stand it anymore. I have to speak to Amanda and tell her about my dreams. Maybe she will help me sort them all out without offending her.

As she comes to see me at my lounger chair, she has a very seductive smile on her face. I start to tell her my night experiences when she places a finger on my lips as if to hush me. I look at her with questions, and she whispers to me to see her after lunch in the massage room, and I can tell her what I want to say then.

After the lunch hour, I look around for Amanda, and she is nowhere to be found, so I decide to go up to the massage room to see if she is there. As I get to the entrance at the top of the stairs I knock on the door and call her name. She responds and invites me in and to wait a minute while she freshens up. I enter the room and notice that she is in her bathroom. After a brief moment, she appears with her bathrobe and apologizes because she just got out of the shower. She walks over to me and, in a gentle tone of voice, asks me what it is I want to tell her. I start to tell her about my erotic dreams, and it appears she is in them. She comes closer to me, and in a very swift movement, she opens her robe, and, at the same time, pushes me against the wall while pinning my wrists to the wall with her hands.

She says, "I know honey all about them, and yes, it is me in your dreams." Baffled as I might be, Amanda stands before me nude, telling me that it is her in my dreams.

"Amanda, what the hell is going on?"

"Shh, now just be quiet, and I will show you."

Amanda places her lips on mine and sticks her tongue into my mouth. I reciprocate. She then lowers herself and unbuttons my pants as she places her hands on my inner thighs. My cock responds and the erection points at her face as she puts me in her mouth and starts stroking me with her lips.

My maleness overtakes me, and I cannot stand it anymore. I lift Amanda's head from my cock and gently push her over to the massage table. I bend her over very lightly as I remove her robe. I don't need to spread her legs too far because of that charming gap between her thighs. I place my finger into her pussy to see if it is wet enough for penetration and find it is very wet. The lubricating discharge is leaking from her cherry very steadily. I grab my cock and tease her vaginal opening with the head until I slowly insert myself completely as her pussy reciprocates, engulfing me with a steady tightness. Slowly, but steadily I thrust in and out while massaging her clit with my finger. I wait until her moans turn into a low scream when I thrust my last as my discharge races into her.

After both Amanda's and my body stops quivering, I ask her why my dreams involved her. She tells me my dreams were not dreams. After every dinner meal, she would drug me by placing powder in my drink and caused me to fall asleep. The dreams were real. She would come into my room and perform all the acts that I was supposedly dreaming.

I ask why she is seducing me, and she tells me she has a lust for sex and looking for the right person to share herself.

Before we get further in the discussion, I have to ask her what she did when I ejaculated on the massage table and if it was the first time she kissed me. She said the only time she kissed me was just when she had me against the wall. She then went on to tell me that she had done '69' on the massage table, and the only lips kissing me were her pussy labia. As soon as she tells me that, I have an immediate erection.

I ask Amanda where we, or she, goes from here.

"I need you, Louie. I need you for sex! I need you for sex all day and every day."

I ask her how she manages throughout the day, and she tells me that she has to masturbate a lot.

I tell her there is no way I can stay at the resort. I have work to get back too, but I am inclined to work out a way to stay because I have become obsessed with her and beginning to feel the same as she does. After all, Amanda is a hot diva, and I can live out my life reasonably well, fucking her every hour of the day.

"Amanda, how did you survive all this time before me? There is no way you masturbated all that time."

"I have had other men, but you...you Louie are the one I want!"

I worked it out with my boss to be able to stay for another couple of weeks. I told him some lame excuse that I couldn't come back right away. So, Amanda and I kept going to the massage room but not for more free massages. In fact, no massages at all. Amanda and I had sex, very intense sex. Frontal entrance, backdoor doggie-style, oral, '69', etc. You name it, and we had it.

Chapter Seven

THE KITCHEN CHEF

*A*fter dinner and before I go up to the massage room for one last romp for the day, the kitchen chef approaches me and tells me she knows what is going on between Amanda and me. She tells me she has seen the scenario many times before me. She says the massage room door hinges are very 'well oiled'. I ask her to explain. She tells me Amanda has had many men just like me and seduces them just as she has me. I ask her where those men have gone, and she says one day they just disappear. When she confronts Amanda about those guys, Amanda tells her they were no good, and all they wanted was her body, so she dropped them.

"Amanda is evil; she is. Haven't you wondered about the color of her eyes? When have you ever seen such color of piercing red in another human being?"

I ask her what she is talking about, and she says, in her opinion, Amanda is some kind of witch.

So Amanda seduces me. So what? I just pass off this conversation as jealousy. The chef probably wishes she could get fucked just as Amanda is fucked by me.

"You just wait and see, buddy. Be careful because soon she is going to catch you in her snatch and never let you go until your cock falls off!"

I reassure her it is between Amanda and me, and it is uninhibited sex, and neither of us wants anything more.

Later, I start to think about what the chef lady had said to me. Was there a meaning when she told me Amanda would cause my cock to fall off? Why did she come up with that fact? Is it because we are having so much sex that we will wear each other out physically? Amanda does have a tight pussy, and she has demonstrated a certain tightness around my cock, but never enough for it to fall off. Hell, I have read that male dogs sometimes will walk around still mounted to the female after connection and ejaculating waiting for the female to release his penis. It is all nonsense. My cock will never fall off by fucking Amanda.

I tell Amanda that I can only stay at the resort for another couple of weeks. I ask her if she will go back with me so we can continue our relationship with sex. She says that it might be a possibility.

One night after our sex routine in the massage room, Amanda tells me that she is going to follow me to my cabin, and she is going to sleep with me. It is the first it was ever suggested. Hell, I figure, why not? We will just have sex all night as well as all day. I am beginning to believe that my cock might just fall off after all. Anyway, Amanda sleeping with me at night becomes the norm. I must admit falling asleep curled up together like two spoons is very relaxing and sexy. I love the smell of her.

One morning, I am conversing with Amanda about my two buddies who were to meet me here at the resort. She mentions a couple of men did show up at the resort but a week before I came. I tell her I looked in the registry book for their names and did not see them listed, so they must have decided not to come. She says maybe those two men were not my friends.

When I am not fucking Amanda, I sometimes go to the Center Hall and sit in my lounger and wonder why my friends never made it to the resort. I also remember that when I signed the registry book, there were no male signatures above my name. I wonder who these two men were that Amanda insisted were here before I showed up.

As soon as I see the chef lady, I ask her about the two men. She tells me two men arrived a week earlier than my arrival. They arrived very late and never signed the registry book because Amanda kept them busy the following day. Come the next morning, and the two men were not to be seen. I ask her how Amanda kept the men busy. She tells me by massages and hiking.

"I will tell you again. Leave Amanda alone. You must leave here before tonight. If you don't, well, it will be the last time your cock will ever enter another pussy," the chef lady relates to me.

I don't understand what she has against Amanda. I am sure it is jealousy. Maybe I should make her feel better and seduce her. She probably hasn't had a good fuck in a long time. Hell, she isn't that bad looking for a cook. I will follow her back to the kitchen.

"Hey, I don't know your name, but I feel you might be a little jealous over Amanda and me. How about you and I go over to my cabin? I can give you something you might have been missing for a long time."

"Listen, mister, I would take you up on it, but I don't want any of

Amanda's juices on me. Shit, your cock has been licking that witch's crotch!"

"Oh, come now, I shower after every encounter with her. You mustn't believe I still have Amanda's discharge on me, do you?"

"Look, if Amanda ever found out that I fucked you, she would kill me. Once you get in Amanda's 'grip,' she won't let go. You are hers now. You must leave here before Amanda seduces you again."

"You think Amanda is a witch?"

"Yes, and I am telling you, she will castrate you!"

"Oh, come on! I never heard of any female castrating a male by fucking. No way can that happen!"

"Well, suit yourself. I wish it were different because I haven't been fucked in many years, and I would love the remembrance of the feeling once again. Now, thanks for the invitation, but heed what I tell you."

After I leave the chef lady, I start to think about Amanda. I want to masturbate thinking about her, but I don't want to waste my load. Suddenly there is a knock at my cabin door.

Chapter Eight

HOT PANTS™

"Louie, you in there? It is I, Amanda. I think we have some catching up to do."

"Yes, honey, I was just thinking of you."

"Give me a half-hour and come on up to my room. I have something special for you."

As I ascend the stairs to the massage room, I can smell the scent of Amanda. It is the same scent I had smelled between her breasts, on her torso, and around her vagina.

"Come on in, Louie."

"Holy shit Amanda, what are those you are wearing?"

"I told you I had a surprise for you. Do you like them?"

I stood there, staring at her. She is wearing very tight 'Hot Pants™', and they are low on her hips, revealing her navel and the start of her pubic hair. The leg openings on those pants go up to her crotch inches away from her opening, and the tightness of those shorts give way to the outline of her labia.

"Damn, Amanda, I love them. I am almost releasing my discharge of semen in my pants. You are some hot bitch. I hate to have you remove them. They are turning me on!"

"Louie, these are special. See, I have a zipper right here in my crotch. You unzip me, and I will be right there to engulf you."

I strip my clothes off and hop on the massage table facing up. I am stiff to the point I believe my cock is two inches longer. Amanda wraps her lips around my shaft and licks it up and down with her tongue, while I reach around and slowly unzip the zipper on her crotch. Instantly her discharge runs over my hand. She hops up on the table; rips her top off, exposing her firm tits and erect nipples. I want to suck them, but she immediately straddles me as she lowers herself onto my cock. Her well-lubricated pussy kisses my shaft as she lowers it onto me until it engulfs me. She then starts the rhythmic motion stroking my shaft. Amanda lowers her torso onto my chest and whispers in my ear.

"So, what did the chef cook tell you about me this afternoon? I saw her and you enter the kitchen this afternoon."

"Oh, she is just jealous that you and I are fucking. I think she wants some of the action."

"Well, Louie, did you take her up on it? Are you cheating on me, Louie?"

"Hell no, Amanda. You are the girl for me. She told me if I fuck you enough, my dick will fall off."

"Did you believe her, Louie?"

"Well, I kind of did, but now after talking to you, I realize she is just a jealous witch."

Chapter Nine

A CUTTING DREAM

"*A*manda, you have such a tight pussy…."

Just as I said that Amanda rolls me on my side and I swear I will fall out of her, but she has my shaft clamped so tight, it stays put just as she wraps her legs around me.

"Amanda, it feels so good, but I think you don't have to grip me that tightly."

There is no response from her as she continues the rhythm of movements. She tightens her legs around me, and I swear her pussy is an extension to her legs because it tightens just as her legs tighten around me. I begin to feel uncomfortable for a moment until I feel my load traveling up my cock as it blasts into her. At that moment, my orgasm is so intense, nothing I have ever experienced before My whole cock and the surrounding area goes numb. I feel warmth running down my leg, which cannot be my load because it surely had hit its target in Amanda. Amanda pulls away from me, and I notice she has blood running down her legs. I look down at myself and notice blood gushing down my legs. I take another glance at Amanda, ready to ask her what happened when I see the unthinkable. Hanging out of her crotch is my cock! She severed my cock, and it is still in her pussy! I scream as the numbness subsides, and the excruciating pain immediately follows all over my lower torso. I look over at Amanda again, her eyes are black and piercing right through me with fire red pupils. She has a sinister smile on her face with her tongue sticking out between her lips.

"Louie, you don't have much time left, but you need to know I appreciate your attention to me while being here at the resort. Do you think I would give you all of those massages for free? You are probably wondering why you lost your cock? These 'Hot Pants™' you adore so much, have a razor type blade sewn behind the zipper. The more I squeeze you with my legs, the more the blade goes clean through your cock. "

"Did the chef cook tell you I was a witch? She tells everyone that. Guess what, Louie? I am a witch...a very jealous witch! You shouldn't have been talking to her. We could have had many more days fucking, but she ruins it every time men come here. She opens her damn mouth and, well...I have to...well, you see what I have to do. I know, Louie, you don't have much time before you bleed to death, and I have to get rid of your body. I have a Yoga class this afternoon and need to get cleaned up."

"Amanda, I never did anything with the chef cook. You are my girl! I did not ask to talk to her."

"You guys never do, Louie."

"Amanda, take me to the hospital. They can sew it back on."

"Even if they could, it will be of no use to me, Louie. It will never become stiff again."

"Amanda, you can at least save my life instead of me bleeding to death."

"Here, Louie, I don't need this anymore."

As I gaze up to her, she pulls my cock out of her pussy and throws it onto my stomach.

"Bye, Louie, it has been great fucking you while it lasted."

"Amanda don't leave me. Please help me....Amanda.....Amanda....nooooo..."

Just at that moment, I quickly sit up in my bed, drenching in sweat.

"Oh, my God! That was just a dream and a very vivid one at that! I wonder if all of this can be true? Is the chef lady correct in what she has told me about Amanda? I need to talk to Amanda…I need to tell her about my dream…or should I? Maybe I should just pack up and leave just like the chef lady told me to do."

I quickly compose myself and leave my cabin to go to the Center Hall and recover in my lounger. I notice not many people are in the Hall this afternoon. The chef lady emerges from the kitchen and sees me in the corner.

"What the hell happened to you? You look like shit, and your facial expression indicates to me that you have seen a ghost or something."

"Well, when you told me about Amanda the other day and said she was a witch, I started thinking about it and must have fallen asleep in my cabin. I had the most vivid dream that Amanda did, indeed, chop off my cock."

"Are you sure it didn't happen?"

"Well, yes, I immediately checked to be sure I still had my cock."

Chapter Ten

THE INVITATION

"Look, I haven't seen Amanda at all today. I have been thinking about your invitation about you and I getting together for a fuck," says the chef.

"Did you think I was serious about that invitation?" asks Louie.

"Well, weren't you?" asks the chef.

"Yes, I guess I was serious. I thought that maybe if I fucked you, it would satiate the jealousy you have for Amanda and me. Besides, you told me you didn't want any of her juices in you from my cock. And what about Amanda? If she were to find out, well, I might as well say goodbye to my cock. I am afraid she will cut it off if she found out I am playing around with you."

"Listen, she doesn't have to know. I won't tell her, and I am sure you won't tell her either," says the chef.

"OK, so what do you want to do?" asks Louie.

"Louie, I want you to fuck me like you do Amanda."

"Well, I, I suppose I could do that. Where and when?"

"Tonight after dinner in my room, which is off of the kitchen."

"Amanda usually wants to screw after dinner and into the night," states Louie.

"Don't worry, Louie. It will work out. At around ten tonight, knock on the kitchen door. Can you do that, Louie?"

"Yes, as long as I am not busy with Amanda."

I walk back to my cabin, wondering how this is all going to work. After all, do I want to fuck the chef lady? She isn't as young and pretty as Amanda, but she isn't bad either. You see one pussy, you have seen them all, I guess. I wonder why she suddenly wants to take me up on fucking her? She was pretty adamant about not having that happen. Maybe she is trying to save me from getting chopped off by Amanda, or perhaps she wants a good screw before I lose my cock. Well, I will have a go of it tonight and see how it turns out.

Chapter Eleven

A NEW GUEST ARRIVES

*A*round nine-thirty, I make my way over to the Center Hall. I am puzzled why I had not seen or heard from Amanda. As I settle into my lounger, I experience a special kind of quiet. There is no one around, and I don't hear any movements in the kitchen area. Suddenly the entrance door to the hall swings open, and a sweet looking sexy thing emerges into the room. She doesn't appear over the age of twenty-five. She has long black hair just like Amanda's and a chiseled face with charming dimples on each cheek. Her eyes are dark, and her lips are plump, black, and inviting. As she walks by me, she looks straight into my eyes and moistens her lips with her tongue in a very seductive manner. She passes me while I am sitting in my lounger and what the hell; she has quite the separation of her thighs as they extend up to her torso. The Yoga Pants™ gives way to her ass, and I can easily see the separation of her labia. She then turns around and faces me.

"Well, hello there. What is your name, dear?" asks Louie.

"My name is Estella. Is there anyone here who can help me? Or maybe you can."

"Well, what is it you would like help?"

"I am looking for the staff to assign me a room at this resort."

"No one is here at the moment. I have been sitting here for about twenty minutes and have not heard or seen anyone. Are you going to be staying for a while?"

"Yes, I will be staying here for a least a month or two; maybe even longer."

"I have an appointment in about ten minutes. It should only be ten or fifteen minutes. You can have a seat in my lounger, here, while you wait. If you are still here when I return, we can take a walk until someone from the staff shows up."

"I hope they show up very soon because I am so tired from the trip and would like to lie down for a while."

"Tell you what. Take this key and head over to my cabin. The bed has clean linens, and I haven't slept there since they were changed. Make yourself at home, and I will see you soon."

"Well, thank you....mister.."

"Louie LaMont."

"So nice to meet you, Mr. LaMont."

"You can call me Louie."

"OK, Louie. Thanks for the invitation to rest in your cabin."

"My pleasure, dear."

Chapter Twelve

ESMERALDA

*A*fter I leave that beautiful girl, Estella, I walk over to the kitchen door and knock a few times on the door.

"Come in Louie. Make yourself at home while I finish freshening up."

As I enter the kitchen, I notice how clean the area is and how every utensil has a place with no clutter on any of the tables.

"By the way, I have been very inconsiderate and never asked you your name."

From the other room off from the kitchen, the chef lady hollers out, "My name is Esmeralda."

"Wow, what a beautiful name!"

"Yes, my momma was very proper and made sure I had a very proper name."

Just as soon as Esmeralda finishes her answer, she emerges from the other room.

"Holy shit! You look beautiful, Esmeralda."

"What did you think, Louie? A lady can be pretty proper and sexy looking when she is on the prowl."

"Are you on the prowl?"

"Yes, I am, and you know it. I know I will never look as beautiful as

Amanda, but I can assure you once I have dropped my clothes, it won't matter. I do believe I have the edge over Amanda in that category."

"Well, we will just have to see about that. I figured you to be at least ten years older than Amanda, but I guess I was wrong."

"Age, Louie. What does that have to do with it?"

As I look up at Esmeralda, I notice that she doesn't look much older than Amanda. She looks much younger than when I first met her a few days ago.

"Come over here, Louie, and untie my laces."

I approach her and reach between her breasts to untie the laced corset she is wearing. I immediately smell a familiar smell radiating from her breasts. It reminds me of Amanda. As I untie the last part of the lacing, her corset opens, and her breasts poke out at me. Her nipples are erect, and I take them in my hands as I lower my mouth to suckle them. Esmeralda reaches down and cups her hands in my groin as the lump in my pants gets larger. I automatically see Amanda in front of me. I quickly pull her corset down to expose her complete breasts and torso. I gently put my hands on her hips and move her to the table. Carefully, but deliberately I push her face down on the table and place my hands on her ass. I push my hands between her thighs under her skirt and search for her clitoris as I spread her labia with my fingers. She has made it easy for me by not wearing panties. She starts moaning seductively as I place myself into her. She starts panting in unison with me as she moves her hips in concert with mine. It doesn't take long before she climaxes, and my cock empties into her. After our bodies stop quivering, I give her a slight tap on her ass with my hand.

"Louie, it has been so long since I felt making love. We will need to do this again. How about this time every other night?"

"I have to make time for Amanda, you know."

"I am sure you will be able to fit me in your schedule."

"I need to get back to my cabin before Amanda shows up and sees me with you. I also need some recuperation time so that I can unload with Amanda."

"OK, Louie, I can't wait till we meet again, goodnight."

"Goodnight, Esmeralda."

Chapter Thirteen

ESTELLA

As soon as I leave the kitchen and enter the Center Hall, I see my lounger empty and no sight of that hot diva I had just met. She must have taken me up on my invite to my cabin. As I open the door to the cabin, I see Estella sound to sleep on the bed. I notice her clothes on the chair, so she must be completely nude under the bed cover. Still aroused by the activity with Esmeralda, I feel a sensation in my groin area, which is screaming for more action. I walk over to the bed and quietly and carefully reach down and grasp the bed cover. I slide it down, exposing her torso to her waist. She is lying on her side, facing away from me, and I see her ample breasts and ass. I peer a little further and see her jet-black pubic hair poking out between her thighs. So as not to wake her, I pull the bed cover back up over her nude body. I place my hand on my groin and try to alleviate the erection but, at the same time, massage the area thinking of Amanda and that hot babe in my bed.

A couple of hours pass and Estella starts to stir from her sleep. She rolls over, facing me with a smile on her face.

"How long have I been asleep?"

"Oh, a few hours, I believe."

"I hope you don't mind me making myself at home in your bed?"

"No, not at all. I am pleased to be able to help. By the way, I still have not seen any staff walking around, and seeing it is past eleven, I am offering you my bed for the rest of the night."

"Where will you sleep, Louie?"

"I will just settle into this chair here."

"Louie, did you happen to pull the cover down to gaze at my body since I am nude under here?"

"Well, I..I."

"Don't worry about it, Louie. I don't mind if you did look."

"It is late, Estella. We will find the staff in the morning so you can get a room."

"Thank you Louie, goodnight."

"Good night, my dear and sweet dreams."

I watch her snuggle down into the bed covers as I turn off the light. There is a slight glow from the embers in the fireplace, which illuminates a soft shadow on Estella's face. She squirms a little as her covers slide down to allow her breasts to peek out at me. Her areola are very dark, and her nipples emerge from the center of them as if at attention.

I settle in the chair, and before long, I, too, fall asleep.

Suddenly, after I had been sleeping awhile, I am awakened enough to see what looks like a silhouette of a female in front of me. The embers from the fireplace are still hot enough to shed a warm light on her. She raises her hand to mine and pulls me toward her. Hand in hand, she leads me to the bed and places her hands on my hips as she swiftly lowers my sweatpants. I lift my legs out of them so as not to trip as she pushes me down on the bed. As I lie there, the silhouette of her arouses me enough, so in the light emitted from the fireplace, I see my cock standing erect in the air from my groin. I soon see her spread a leg over me until she is straddling me. She is blocking the light emitting from the fireplace so I can no longer see her silhouette. I feel a warm and moist gripping on my cock, and then the sliding up and down my shaft. I reach for her hips as she grabs my hands and pushes my arms up over my head and pins them down to the bed mattress.

I start to think about Amanda. I have had three women who have fucked me. I can't say that I am disappointed, but am I going to have to fuck or be fucked by every female that comes to the resort?

Once Estella has massaged my shaft enough to spew my load into her, she hops off of me and settles into the bed under the covers. She slides herself to me until her ass presses on my groin and pulls my arms around her and places my hands on her breasts. I put her nipples between my fingers and gently squeeze them with a slight tugging motion. She starts to moan, and I can feel her thighs begin to spread in a position that allows me to reach down while I slide my finger through her labia to find the target enabling her to orgasm several times.

I awaken in the morning by the sunlight that comes through the window over the bed. I realize Estella is not beside me, and her clothes are no longer on the chair. I am not sure how I am going to explain the soiled sheets to Amanda when she comes to change the linens. She will know those stains weren't from her, and there is too much of it to be just a 'wet dream'.

After showering and dressing, I walk over to the Center Hall for breakfast. As I open the door and start to walk over to my lounger chair, Estella is sitting next to the table on the couch. She is wearing a pair of Hot Pants™ that shows her slender and well-toned legs from her ankles to her crotch. The shorts are so tight I can see the separation of her labia as she sits with her legs slightly apart.

As far as her torso goes, she is wearing a loose-fitting halter style top giving way to her nude midriff and navel. Again, I feel the urge to stick my tongue into her navel.

The halter-style top material is very sheer, and I see her dark areola showing ever so slightly through. Her nipples are still quite erect. Looking at her arouses me to the point of making my sitting in my lounger uncomfortable. She looks over to me and parts her lips moistening them with her tongue while spreading her legs a little wider.

"Are you afraid Amanda will find out how I fucked you last night?"

"Well, I am concerned. It was you? How do you know about Amanda?"

"Oh, it doesn't matter. Amanda will be back tonight. I guess I won't have you tonight with her arrival. Of course, we could get together before she returns," says Estella.

"How do you know I am with Amanda?" asks Louie.

"Oh, you mean fucking her? Everybody fucks her."

Just as I am about to inquire more about how Estella knows Amanda and our sexual encounters, Esmeralda emerges from the kitchen. She immediately glances at Estella, and I see a look come over her face, much like a cat when about to enter into a fight. Estella looks at Esmeralda, and I swear she reciprocates with a hissing sound. Well, they say you can't have 'two women in the kitchen at the same time'. I wonder if each of them knows they are both fucking me, and that is why the 'cat fight'?

Chapter Fourteen

CAT FIGHT AND THE THREE

*A*s I watch the sneering between the two ladies, the Center Hall door opens, and three more girls enter. Hell, each of them don't look over twenty-five in age just like Estella. They all look very similar and have jet black hair and eyebrows with blackened pupils in their eyes and black lipstick. They all have black fingernail polish. I look over at Estella and, for the first time, notice her nail polish is black as well. The funny thing is, all of these girls have body proportions similar to that of Estella and are very 'hot' looking. I immediately start thinking that I will be fucking them in time. What the hell is going on here? I haven't seen any men here since I came to the resort, only women…'hot' women. As each of the girls pass by me, they glance at me, all moistening their lips with their tongues.

I eat my breakfast without interacting with any of the girls and return to my cabin to think about what is happening with these strange circumstances. All of these women or girls, or at least the three of them, appear to want to be fucked and be fucked often. I seem to be the participant who is to satisfy them. I am not complaining, but if this keeps up and if these three new ladies who just showed up want to be serviced, my cock won't be chopped off, but fall off due to overuse. I am going to have to leave here soon. I am sure I can't convince my boss I need to stay here longer, but I don't know if these ladies will allow me to leave.

Suddenly there is a knock on my cabin door.

"Come on in. The door is open. Oh, hello, Amanda. I thought you were not to return until later tonight."

"How did you know this, Louie?"

"Well, the ladies over there in the hall…"

"Oh, you mean that witch in the kitchen?"

"Well, her and the others that have come here recently. Do you know we now have four more women here?"

"Yes, I have seen them. So, let's forget those bitches and talk about us."

Chapter Fifteen

REUNITING

"*A*manda, I have missed you so much, and I have a lot to tell you."

"Let's hold that for a while and you come up to my room in about fifteen minutes. We have a lot of catching up to do. Be ready because I am super-horny, and I need you to reciprocate."

"Oh, Amanda, I can do that for you. I have missed you, your smell, and your sweet wet pussy. I hope you don't mind if I get a little rough with you."

"Louie, I expect you to fuck me hard! Now get ready. I will be waiting for you in my room in ten minutes."

"Amanda, I hope…."

"Louie, don't worry. I will."

I wonder how she knows what I was about to ask. Woman's intuition, I guess. I won't worry about not putting my undershorts on when I dress. They just get in the way. I will take a shower to get Estella's scent off of me. I am sure Amanda can tell another female's scent on me. I sure as hell don't want her to feel any kind of jealousy. I don't want to encourage dismemberment. I also have to decide how I can approach relaying my dream to Amanda.

"Come in Louie! I will be out in a minute."

"Holy shit, Amanda!"

"What is the matter, Louie? You don't like what you see?"

"Yes, I do. You look so hot in those Hot Pants™ I can hardly stop discharging semen in my pants."

"How about these, Louie"

"My God, they look more beautiful than the last time I saw them."

"Well, come over here and uncover me so you can see more."

I immediately rush over to her and pull her top off in a slightly rough manner. I cup her tits in my hands and run my fingers over her already erected nipples. Right after I tug on them, Amanda starts moaning, and she reaches for my head to push my lips over her nipples. I immediately start sucking them while pulling on them with my lips. Amanda drops her hands down to my waist and lowers my pants. My cock raises in stiffness as she lowers herself to place her lips around my shaft. She immediately strokes me in a vivacious manner.

"Amanda, slow down. I don't want to cum in your mouth."

"Why not, Louie?"

"I want to experience the tightness of your pussy. I want my tongue to wallow in your wetness and taste your discharge," states Louie.

I roughly push Amanda away from my cock; pick her up at the waist and rush her over to the massage table and remove her 'Hot Pants™'. I gently push her torso face down. Looking at her bare ass, I see her lubricating discharge running down her inner thighs. I quickly bend down and place my tongue between her labia to taste and smell her and then follow the release down her legs, licking and swallowing. After I roughly thrust my cock into her pussy, I come to orgasm quickly. She rolls over and grabs my still stiff cock and places its head on her clitoris. She rhythmically moves it over her labia and up to her sensory clit until she experiences multiple orgasms. Not being satisfied, I pull away from her and lower my face to her pussy while inhaling her smell and licking her discharge. I dance around her clit with my tongue to give her another round of orgasms. She finally gets her way and quickly grabs my cock and pushes it through her lips and into her mouth. The sensation I realize as she vigorously sucks and squeezes with her lips while running up and down my shaft makes me forget about insisting on ejaculating in her pussy. As she engulfs my entire cock in her mouth, I start to feel my load, once again, move towards its exit until I can no longer hold it, and it blasts into her mouth. Amanda immediately swallows my load and then continues to lick the rest off of my shaft with her tongue.

Chapter Sixteen

THE CROTCH ZIPPER

When we are done fucking, and while we rest in each other's arms waiting for our bodies to stop quivering, she asks me how I had managed while she was gone. I start by telling her about my dream and pointing out I was scared when I saw her in the 'Hot Pants™' hoping I didn't lose my cock.

"Louie, where did you get that idea from?"

"The kitchen chef told me. Remember I told you about her telling me you are a witch and you will chop me…"

"Oh, I thought I put that out of your mind. I will put that to rest when I see Esmeralda."

"Amanda, would you mind if I take a look at your Hot Pants™?"

"To see what? A zipper in my crotch with a razor type knife under the zipper?"

"Yeah, if you wouldn't mind."

"Have at it, Louie. Don't forget to sniff the crotch."

"Oh, I won't. That is some of the reason I want to see those pants."

"OK, Louie, what did you find? Is there a zipper in the crotch of my pants?"

"Well, yes, there is!"

"How about a razor type knife?"

"No, there is not one of those that I can see."

"OK, so does that set your mind at ease?"

"Do you have another pair or pairs of Hot Pants™?"

"Yes, I do. Go ahead and check them all out. Now look, Louie, I will need you back here after dinner, say around ten, and we will continue our so-called 'fuckfest'."

"OK, Amanda."

"Get going Louie, I have a few things to do before dinner."

"Oh, Amanda, I am sorry about my linens. You will see some of my 'wet dreams' have stained them more than usual. I had missed you so much; I had to masturbate so that you will see quite a large amount."

"Don't worry about it, Louie. I will take care of it."

I feel less stressed about the soiled linens from Estella and me fucking earlier. Amanda can't know I fucked Estella. She can't even know I fucked Esmeralda, and she can't find out I will probably fuck the other girls that just arrived, because I know it will happen sooner or later. These ladies, here at the resort, all appear to be well-established whores.

Chapter Seventeen

AMANDA IS CORDIAL

*A*manda goes from the cabin straight to the Center Hall. As she enters the Hall, she introduces herself to the new girls.

"Hello, all. My name is Amanda, and I welcome you to the resort. During your stay here, there are some rules."

"Where is the staff?" asks Estella.

"The staff is not here at the moment, so you will be dealing with me on all matters. I will be handing out your keys to your rooms this afternoon. In case you have not noticed, we have a male guest here at the resort. He is staying in the cabin. He is here for relaxation, and I would hope you honor his relaxation time here. You will see him frequent my room quite often because he has scheduled numerous massages. You, too, may want to schedule massages as well. Again, I hope you enjoy your stay here, and if you have any questions about anything, please do not hesitate to ask me."

Chapter Eighteen

ESMERALDA IS WARNED

manda leaves the girls and marches to the kitchen.

"Esmeralda, what the hell are you telling Mr. LaMont? He told me that you told him I would chop off his 'dick' if he kept fucking me. He also insists that you told him I am a witch."

"You are, Amanda."

"I want you to stay away from Mr. LaMont, or there will be consequences, and you do not want those."

"Amanda, what do you think you can do to me? You don't have any power over me."

"I am warning you, Esmeralda!"

"How long do you think you can continue fucking him, Amanda, before he finds out the truth?"

"Who I fuck and when I fuck is no business of yours."

"Well, I hope your pussy rots and then…"

"And then what, Esmeralda? Do you think you could get in on the action? Don't bet on it! You couldn't give him half of what I can and do give him! Be careful, and you just might find that your pussy has completely dried up, and nothing can slide in or out of it."

"Yeah, sure, Amanda. Are you going to do something about that?"

"Don't tempt me, Esmeralda. As I said, mind your own business and don't go near Mr. LaMont!"

Chapter Nineteen

3:30 IN THE MORNING

I have a couple of hours before my next rendezvous with Amanda. I think I will just sit here on the bed and rest a while. Just as I sit back and relax against the head of the bed, there is a knock on my cabin door.

"Who is it? The door is open."

As the door opens, one of the new girls emerges. Oh, no, I am thinking. Now is not the time for fucking. I have to be with Amanda, and I don't want to be dry.

"How can I help you, sweetheart?"

"My name is Eunice, and you might not have noticed I was one of the three girls arriving earlier today."

"Yes, it was hard not seeing you or the other girls for that matter. You and the other ladies are all gorgeous."

"Yes, that is why I am here. I have a proposition for you. The girls and I are having a contest of who can get fucked by you first. You know, they all want to be fucked and you being the only male here, well, you are the candidate. Of course, they do not know, but I beat them to it, so what do you say? We can do it here or out in the woods or wherever. You will be well pleased when you fuck me because I am a virgin, and my pussy is tight. You see, I don't masturbate with anything stuck up there."

"Interesting, so you don't masturbate? Will I have to teach you how to fuck?"

"Hell no! You needn't worry. I am going to teach you how to fuck a woman properly."

"Oh, I see. Well, I will have to think about it. Maybe I would like to select one of the other girls first."

"Nope, you can't do that. The rules are 'first come, first served', and I am the first-come. Would you like to see what I have to offer right here and now? I will strip right down, right here, right now."

"No, that will be fine. I can tell just by looking at you that you have something special to offer me. You had better keep your pants on for now because I have another commitment this evening."

"Oh, with who? Amanda?"

"How do you know, Amanda?"

"Everyone knows Amanda and what she is and what she does."

"Oh yeah! What is Amanda? A witch? I heard that from the kitchen chef," says Louie.

"The kitchen chef? Esmeralda is a witch!"

"All you women around here are calling each other witches."

"That's because we are."

"Women, I will never figure them out. Always calling each other witches."

"Well, think what you want, but we are," says Eunice.

"OK, OK, can I take a raincheck for tomorrow?" asks Louie.

"Well, let's see. You fuck her later tonight. You should be ready again around 3:00 or 4:00 in the morning. I will be here at 3:30 tomorrow morning."

"Wait a minute! In the early morning? I will be half asleep," says Louie.

"Once I strip down, you will wake up real fast. Make sure you shower after fucking Amanda. I like her, but not that intimately."

"Wha...how do you know.....Amanda?"

"Skip it, Mr. LaMont. Just be ready at 3:30 AM tomorrow."

"We are going to do it here?"

"This place is just as good as any. Be sure to get those linens changed before I get here. I don't fuck with someone else's stains on the linens."

She leaves as fast as she arrived. What the hell and who the hell is she? She is the forward type. A witch? You have to be kidding me. Although the feisty nature, I bet she is quite excellent in bed, and I will bet she does have a tight pussy. Oh well, we will see. I have to get ready for Amanda.

The fuck with Amanda was sensational. Each got better than the previous one. Of all of the girls, women, witches, or whatever they are, Amanda is at the top of the list for giving the most satisfying fuck.

I guess I had better get to bed right away, so I will be 'up' at 3:30 in the morning. I think that I better take a shower. Knowing that babe, she will sniff my cock to see if she can smell Amanda's scent on me.

While sleeping, I have a dream. The babe shows up at my doorstep at 3:30 AM and low and behold the other two are with her. The rest is all just a blur, and I am surprised I didn't have a 'wet dream'; that babe has quite the young pussy she said she has.

A knock at the door startles me, and I glance at my watch. Yup, it is 3:30 AM on the dot.

"Come on in Eunice. I have been waiting for you."

As the door opens, Eunice and the other two girls are with her, just like the dream I had earlier.

"Well, Eunice, how does the contest work when all of you show up?"

"Well, you see, I am the one who gets to fuck first, and then it is up to them who has you next."

"What the hell is this? Do you think I am a whore?"

"No, we are the whores, and you are just the catalyst to get us off. Now, this here is Janice, and she is Johanna."

"More common names for those two, huh?"

"Yeah, they are the young ones. Eighteen and nineteen, to be exact. I am twenty-two. They will be watching to see how it is done."

"An orgy? Good, I hope they enjoy watching."

"They will enjoy watching, but don't overestimate them. Theses bitches are women, and they know how to handle a man."

"Tell me, Eunice, your desires? Doggy, missionary…."

"I will determine that. Just lie down here. Girls tie his wrists to the bedposts and his ankles down here. Now strip him down to his waist but do not touch him. That is my job. Oh, and put this gag in his mouth. I don't want Amanda hearing his hollering."

"What kind of orgy is this Eunice?" asks Louie.

"Shut up and enjoy the ride."

Once I am tied down, and the gag is placed in my mouth, all three girls strip down until they are all nude. Being young girls, I can see they are well developed beyond their age. Looking at the three of them, I can't help but get an erection at 3:30 in the morning. Eunice pulls my sweatpants down to my knees. Immediately my cock stands erect, and Eunice grabs hold of the shaft and starts stroking it. The other two girls take their turns, placing their tits on my mouth, and what the hell, I suckle each one of them. Janice hops on me and settles herself over my face. I can smell the familiar scent of a well-moistened pussy.

Just as I get my tongue out of my mouth, Janice hops off me, and Johanna jumps on over my face. Neither of them will let me place my tongue in their pussies. One after the other teases me with their moves over my face. I am so busy with these two girls trying to get a lick that I don't recognize Eunice has engulfed my cock within her and starts to move to allow it to slide in and out. All of a sudden, just before I empty into Eunice, one of the girls wafts a cloth over my nose. The smell is quite pleasant, almost like that of sage. I feel lightheaded and start to succumb to sleep. What happened after that I do not know, but when I woke up, I looked at the linen, other than some semen stains, there are plenty of different stains. I leaned down and smelled them. Sure enough, the soil smelled like pussy. I guessed with the three of them; there was a lot of juices flowing. I believe they each had a chance at riding my shaft, although I do not know how. After one fuck, I am usually suitable for another shot but have to wait for some time after for another. I do feel a little raw down there. The drug they gave me to fall asleep must have also been the cause of a sustained erection. I wonder what they did to me.

Chapter Twenty

AMANDA EXPLAINS

*O*h, hell, it is six in the morning. Those whores had been with me for two whole hours. There is no way I can show for breakfast. I am so beat and tired.

"Louie, you in there?"

"Whaa.wha..who is there?"

"It is me, Amanda. I need to talk to you. Why haven't you come to breakfast?"

"Amanda, I am not feeling well, and I am exhausted. I can't service your needs this morning."

"Listen, Louie. I am not here begging for you to service me at this moment. I need to talk to you. There is something you need to know, and I think you are in danger."

"In danger? What are you talking about, Amanda?"

"Let me in, and I will tell you all about it."

"The door is open. Come on in."

"Louie, you look like shit."

"I feel like shit. They really did me over."

"Louie, who did you over? Were they here…the three of them?"

"Do you know about them, the three sexy vixens? I am sorry, Amanda. I didn't do it on purpose."

"Can I open a window, Louie? This place smells like pussy and sage."

"Sure, go ahead."

"Louie, I am going to tell you something that has been going on. You won't believe it, but you must know. Esmeralda says I am a witch, and she is correct in that."

"Whaaa…whaaaa?"

"Let me finish Louie. All of the females here at the resort this moment are witches."

"Real witches? I mean those who cast spells?"

"Well, not exactly like that, but very close. I am a descendant of an ancient witch coven at least one hundred or more years back. My ancestors were not witches who cast spells or anything like that, but they did have special powers, special powers involving mind control. They could persuade a person to do things without them even knowing it. One day one of the members of the coven, a male, broke into a sixteen-year-old virgin's bedroom and raped her. The man was put to death, but the girl kept the baby. When her baby grew to be a young woman, it was found that she suffered from nymphomania."

"What the hell is that?"

"Louie, let me finish. Nymphomania is a condition known as sex addiction. She had to have sex to satiate her appetite. She would do anything to have sex, even if it was two to three times a day. Unfortunately for her, the side effects of this addiction and probably because of how she had conceived was to kill the male that she had sexual relations. No one knew what to do with her, and by the time they decided to end her life, she had become pregnant with many babies through time. The sex addiction seed had spread to many females as well as the powers of the witch, getting it from the warlock who had raped her. I am a descendant of hers, and I am a witch, and I am a nymphomaniac. I have to have sex to survive, and yes, I also have killed my partners. Then you came along, and I felt something for you that I never have with all of the other male partners. I am inclined to do away with you, but I just can't."

"That sure as hell is a relief. So you do have a pair of 'Hot Pants™'

with a zippered crotch and razor type blades? Your partners just bleed to death?"

"No, Louie, I do not own a pair of pants like that. You know that! You searched my entire closet and drawers and did not find them. I won't go into how I had killed them, but it was during a sexual encounter, and by way of your dream, I think you know how they were killed. You see, the affliction has to do with retribution for the male warlock raping the girl, and that act along with the retribution has followed throughout the generations. I won't kill you, Louie. I can't because I love you. Somehow meeting you caused some sort of mutation with the affliction in me."

"Yeah, but did you pass it down to one of your illegitimate daughters?"

"No, Louie, I have never been pregnant. I can't get pregnant. I took care of that so I wouldn't contribute to this curse for future genera-tions. But, I must warn you, female witches are wandering around; the descendants with the affliction that have not been exposed to love such as I have. So, as I said at the beginning of this conversation, all of the other females at this resort are witches; descendants from the rape years ago. These women and girls have a special power given to them from this affliction years ago to be able to find men to have sex with. They can feel it inside them like a GPS and search them out."

"Yeah, but there are men all over. I don't see why they need to search."

"Louie, they search because it has to be a special type of male. They have to be males who have no problem with coupling up with numerous women and will have sex with them at their calling. You, Louie, are such a male. I knew you were coming to the resort, so I just waited until you arrived. Your buddies were here, and they talked a lot about you and how much of a 'Casanova' you are."

"So, you killed them, Amanda? You had sex with them and killed them?"

"No, it wasn't me. I wanted to wait for you. Esmeralda killed them after she wore them out, having sex with them. The three vixens who just arrived here are witches in search of you. Now that they have found you, they lured you into having sex with them. Luckily, they didn't kill you this morning."

"You knew about what happened at 3:30 this morning, Amanda?"

"Yes, but it happened before I could do anything about it, and I know they will strike again, and they will kill you. I think because those girls are so young and naive, they enjoy playing a bit with you, and when they have had their fill, they will do away with you, especially should another male show up at the resort."

"Where is the staff that was here when I arrived? Where did they go? They were female, so they weren't murdered, were they?"

"No, the staff here were also witches, and they left to search for their males. You see, this resort has not had staff who aren't witches for some time. They knew better to mess with you on your arrival because they knew I selected you, and by selecting you, I have become your protector. The only problem is the young ones. They have renewed energy, and it is hard for me to steer them away from you. They know my power, so they make use of their energy together when they can, thus the three of them taking you on this morning."

"I am so sorry, Amanda, for allowing them to have at me. I want only you. You must believe me."

"You can't help it because of the power we witches have over you males. We draw you in without you even knowing it. The only thing I can fault you with is your willingness to get pussy, however you can, although I am not complaining too much about that."

"What do I do now, Amanda? I can't leave. I won't leave without you! You need to come with me."

"Yes, that is a problem. I can't leave here because I need to keep these witches at bay and any others that come here when males show up at the resort. You see, I do not want this curse to continue. It is such a wretched curse given so many years ago."

"Why don't you just close down the resort and kill all witches that might show up here?"

"I can't kill them. We all have power in us that will not allow us to hurt one another. It is another curse of being a witch."

"Then how did that warlock years ago get killed after the rape?"

"The girl raped was not a witch, so she was able to kill him, but his seed gave her a baby that had the witches powers, and the baby became a witch. The mother who was raped could not take it upon herself to kill her daughter, and then descendants spread very rapidly after that. Look, Louie, those three girls will be back, and I would guess they will come back unannounced during the night. They will drug you and who knows what they will do to you after they have their fun with you. I also caution you about Esmeralda. She is very dangerous. Don't fall for her if you can help it. Her power is quite strong."

"I am sorry, Amanda, but I did one time."

"Stay away from her! She isn't going to play with you like those others. She will kill you! The only reason she didn't kill you then is because she knew I was coming back and did not know when. I do have powers over her even though she swears I do not. She is getting stronger, and it won't be long before her powers are just as strong as mine, and then I won't be able to control her."

"Why don't I just kill all of them? I am not a warlock. If I kill them, it would be just you and me."

"That would only work for a short period. Others will come because you are here, Louie."

"I don't get it, Amanda. How come I have never been exposed to this back home. Don't you think these witches are all over? Why aren't they doing this all over the place?"

"It is possible, but there is one more thing I haven't told you. This resort is ancient, and it happens to be the center of the coven where the rape occurred. You have heard the saying, 'the chickens come home to roost'?"

"Yes, I have."

"They will come back here; their 'ancient home base' so to speak."

"Let's burn it down. Those witches won't have a place to come back to for their sinister deeds. Sooner or later, those witches and the curse would die out."

"I can't, nor can you now I am involved with you. If you or I were to burn this place down, I would immediately die along with you. I cannot let that happen."

"But I am not a warlock. I have no ties to the witchery."

"Oh, but you have Louie. You have copulated with me, and now you have some of the powers of the witch you don't know."

"How did that happen, Amanda?"

"You and I exchanged bodily fluids many times. You even swallowed much of my discharges during our encounters. You are part of me; part of the witchery in a minimal way."

"What are we to do?"

"Let me think about it, Louie. If you can get your mind away from this for a moment, I need you right now. Lie down here, Louie, while I get you ready to fuck me."

———

I must say that fuck was a little different since Amanda told me about her and the others. Not that I didn't enjoy it, and it didn't stop me from swallowing more of her sweet and salty lubrication, but it was different for sure.

Chapter Twenty-One

HE IS OFF LIMITS

"*E*smeralda, Janice, Eunice, and Johanna, please meet me in the Center Hall. We have some things to sort out. I already warned you, Esmeralda, to stay away from Mr. LaMont, and that still goes. Eunice, I know what you and the rest of you did early this morning."

"Oh, come on, Amanda, we were just having fun. Three on a guy is exciting…."

"Listen, all of you bitches! Stay away from Mr. LaMont! He is mine and all mine."

"Oh come now, Amanda. There are no other males here for us to satiate our lust. You know we have to have it."

"Johanna and the rest of you, would you be satiated by playing with me?"

"How can that be, Amanda? You don't have a 'dick'."

"Well, I believe Esmeralda has figured it out, haven't you? Certain fruits or vegetables are your best friend. Am I correct in saying that, Esmeralda?"

"Amanda, it works for a short time, but if we don't get males here and soon, Mr. LaMont will have to be shared by all of us, and I don't know what we will do when he is dead. You know we have to kill him in the end?"

"What good are fruits and vegetables, Esmeralda?" asks Janice.

"Janice, you naive bitch, you take a banana or a cucumber and slide that baby up between your legs while you rock it back and forth and in and out until you have an orgasm."

"That does not sound like much fun."

"Listen all of you! You will stay away from Mr. LaMont, or you will be sorry!"

"What are you going to do with us, Amanda? You can't do anything to us! We will fuck your man when we want, and you cannot do anything about it," says Johanna.

Amanda lets out a hiss with her teeth bared as she slaps Johanna across her face and lifts her hand to the rest of them.

"Don't try me! I still have power over you all. You will pay if you fuck Mr. LaMont!"

Chapter Twenty-Two

THE DREAM THAT BECAME A DEADLY REALITY

*A*s I sit in my cabin, I hear raised voices coming from over in the Center Hall and hissing like there is a passel of cats over there. Amanda hisses; I have witnessed that. She is not quite human. I do not fear for my life with her, but I indeed fear for my life with the others, especially those young bitches. I try to stay awake as long as I can to be on guard for what might happen. It is midnight, and I can't keep my eyes open any longer, and sleep overcomes me. I start to dream.

"Hello, Mr. LaMont. It is Eunice."

"How did you get into my cabin?"

"Silly you, the door is always unlocked. You can guess why I am here, and I am here alone this time. I will have you all to myself."

"No, no, go away from me, Eunice. I don't want to fuck you."

"But I want to fuck you! Did Amanda fill your head with untruths about me? In case you don't realize it, Amanda is at least ten years older than I am, and she isn't a virgin when you first fucked her. Remember, I was a virgin, and you were the first male I ever fucked. You were able to feel inside my pussy like no man ever has. You and I are one. She is a worn-out whore. You will come to believe me in a short time. I bet she told you I am a witch. I told you that this morning. Now, do you believe me?"

"Amanda told me all about the curse you bitches are bringing with you. She told me that you fuck, and then you kill most bizarrely."

"Oh, Mr. LaMont don't you see, she only is saying that because she wants you all to herself?"

"Eunice, please leave! I don't want anything to do with you. All three of you forced yourselves on me. I didn't ask you to fuck me."

"Come on, Mr. LaMont. You know you loved it. We know what kind of man you are…"

"Eunice! Do not start undressing. I told you I want nothing to do with you witches."

"It is too late for that, Mr. LaMont. You are part of us now. I have the feeling that you have planted something inside me. An offspring to carry the legacy of our ancestry."

"How do you know that? It can't be. When you practically raped me, I just came from being with Amanda. I was spent. You didn't get anything from me."

"Mr. LaMont, I induced a drug that caused you to perform for us. I was very fertile at the time, you know. So now that you know you are the father of my baby, start acting like a partner and lay down here and give me more."

"No, Eunice! Get the fuck out of here. I am not the father of your little witch! There is no way you know this early that you are pregnant. I am not falling for that."

"Listen, you bastard! Lay down on the bed. We are going to fuck whether you want to or not!"

As soon as she makes that statement, I see her eyes turn pitch black, and then her pupils light up with fiery red color. I can't look away like she is casting some kind of spell over me. She comes closer to me, and I can smell the familiar aroma; sage, I believe. Suddenly fear takes over me as I see her drop her skirt and discover she was wearing 'Hot Pants™' not like Amanda's but more like what I had a dream about. No, this can't be happening. Amanda warned me about the ritual, and the dream I had, was real, except the one wearing the pants is not Amanda.

I can't resist Eunice because of the drug she is giving me through that aroma of sage just like she did before, except something is different now. I can sense her hoping on me and unzipping my pants. I can feel her pussy grip around my shaft, and I am conscious. I try to move; try to push her off me, but I have no strength. After a few strokes on my shaft, she hops off me to apply some sort of cream on my cock.

"I beg you. Please stop what you are doing, Eunice. Please take off your pants. Don't fuck me with those pants on."

"Mr. LaMont, you don't like my pants? Don't you think I am sexy in these? I don't need to take them off. Look, I have a zipper in the crotch. All I need to do is unzip...."

"No! No! You mustn't! I don't want my 'dick' cut off and left to die bleeding to death."

"Did Amanda tell you another lie about me? Don't be silly. I just want to get fucked."

Eunice once again hops on me and settles her ass down on me as her pussy licks my cock as it becomes engulfed within her. Suddenly I feel slight numbness in my groin, and it becomes difficult for me to know whether I am in her or not or whether she is stroking me except I can see her ass rhythmically moving in an up and down motion.

"Please stop! It is getting a little too tight! Please release me!"

"Mr. Lamont, quiet down now. You will be all right. Now kiss me."

While she is straddling me, I feel her knees pressing against my waist.

"Eunice, I beg of you! Release your legs. I am afraid...No...No... No! Ahh..."

I blacked out for a while. I didn't see her move off me. The pain is excruciating. There isn't much time before life will flow out of me. I look down, and what I see makes me realize I am not dreaming, and this whole ordeal is a reality. She has chopped off my cock, and I am going to die.

"Mr. Lamont! Here, I don't need this now. You can have it back."

I watch as Eunice pulls my cock from within her and throws it on my chest.

"Why, oh why did you have to do this to me?"

"Mr. LaMont, you know all about the curse. Amanda told you all about it. It is too bad she wouldn't carry out her end of the bargain. She fucked you, and she was supposed to kill you. Instead, she forced me to do it."

"Listen, Eunice. Get me to the hospital. At least you can save my life."

"But I can't, Mr. Lamont. You have to die in this manner. It is the curse, and the curse has to be carried out for generations to come. Don't worry; it won't be long now. You must be quite numb down there by now."

"You young bitch! You…you…I am fading rapidly. Help me….help me…."

"Goodbye, Mr. LaMont."

Eunice walks back to the Center Hall. The crotch of her pants oozing with blood, Louie's blood.

"It is done. Now the three of us must take the body and bury it up on the hill before Amanda finds out. The excuse will be we saw Mr. LaMont leave in his car this morning and that he took all of his clothes with him," states Eunice out loud.

"Should we tell Esmeralda what I did? I am sure she will be pleased the curse is living on," says Eunice.

"No, she will know in time. We have to convince Amanda that he just left. It will be easier if just the three of us know the truth."

"Eunice, was it rather easy. I mean, did he suffer much?" asks Janice.

"Nah, he was quite numb down there. Now quick, help me get him up the hill. After we bury him, we need to strip his bed linens and bury those as well. We need to scrub all blood stains from the cabin, and I need to bury these pants and take a shower."

Chapter Twenty-Three

LIES, DECEPTION AND SORROW

*A*manda enters the Center Hall looking for Louie. She wants to talk to him about a plan to escape, just the two of them.

"Has anyone seen Mr. LaMont this morning?"

"No, we haven't," responds Janice and Johanna in unison.

"I saw him this morning just as he was leaving in his car. I rushed over to his cabin, and all of his clothes and belongings are gone. I think he left to go back to his home," responds Eunice.

"Eunice, come over here! I am sensing something. Yes, the aroma of sage!" exclaims Amanda.

"Yes, I love sage. I have a sage body wash."

"Eunice, you and I know what the powers of sage are if used in the wrong way. It is unfortunate Eunice you weren't taught how to sit properly like a lady while wearing a skirt. Of course, whores don't care what is showing; no panties with a visible snatch; one of your calling cards, I suppose," states Amanda.

Amanda walks over to where Eunice is sitting and places her leg forward between Eunice's open knees and pushes one from the other.

"Eunice, it looks as if you forgot to use your sage body wash down there. Of all places! You reek of pussy, and what is with all the blood on your inner thighs up to your crotch?"

"Amanda, you know, I have my period, and I meant to take a shower, but I ran out of time."

"That is a lie, Eunice! The blood you have on you is not from your so-called menstrual cycle. You were with Mr. LaMont this morning, weren't you?"

"No, I tell you I have my period, and it is leaking much more than usual this month."

Suddenly Amanda's eyes become as dark as night, and her pupils radiate a fiery red color while staring directly at Eunice.

"You bitch! You carried out the curse on Mr. LaMont! You killed him, didn't you? You cut off his penis and left him to bleed to death. That blood is Mr. LaMonts' and not your so-called period of which you do not have!"

Amanda's eyes start to water, and tears start running down her cheeks.

"I did what you were supposed to do, Amanda. You were the one who fucked him first; many times, I am sure!"

"Shut up, you slut! You will pay for this. You will all pay for this!"

"Oh, Amanda, there is nothing you can do to us now," says Esmeralda.

"Yeah, we all got at least one fuck out of him while he was here," says Johanna.

"Yeah, and I am going to have his baby!" exclaims Eunice.

"You will never see that baby, Eunice!"

"There is nothing you can do about it, Amanda."

"That baby was to be mine!" exclaims Amanda.

"Aw, poor Amanda! You know you are too dried up to be fertile!" exclaims Esmeralda.

Chapter Twenty-Four

RETRIBUTION

$\mathcal{A}$manda, with a full downpour of tears, rushes swiftly out of the Center Hall and runs up to her room. She throws herself on the bed wishing she had taken Louie up on his insistence of leaving the resort right away. After a while, she forces herself to decide how she will take retribution.

At eleven that night, when she is sure all will be asleep, she travels to the shed where all of the lawn care items are kept. Back at the resort, she goes from one room to the next and soaks the curtains with gasoline. She goes up to her room and douses everything and then makes a trail down the steps and across the room to the basement stairway. Once in the basement, she empties the rest of the gasoline near and at the bottom of the furnace.

Once the fire is underway, she knows she must work fast to get up the hill to Louie's burial site.

Just as Amanda leaves the Center Hall, she turns the furnace thermostat up to start the furnace in approximately ten minutes. She walks over to the cabin where Louie was staying and rushes over to his bed, where his blood had stained the linens. Amanda falls onto the bed and buries her face in the pillow where Louie last placed his head. A loud wale of despair emits from her mouth as once again, she bawls.

"I love you, Louie."

It didn't take long for the entire resort to burst into flames. Amanda watches out the cabin window hoping not to see any of the women escaping from the infernal. Fifteen minutes is all the time needed for the resort to become a pile of embers.

Chapter Twenty-Five

I LOVE YOU LOUIE

*A*manda rushes out of the cabin and heads to the hill where Louie is buried. When she arrives, she falls onto the mound of ground covering Louie. She wraps her arms as if to be hugging him and moves her entire body on top of the mound. She starts chanting how much she loves Louie.

"Louie, I am so sorry. I love you...I love you. Louie, I am so sorry. I love you...I love you!"

Amanda anticipates her fate and waits for the fiery blast. The flames swiftly engulf her until there is just a charred corpse lying on top of Louie's grave.

Chapter Twenty-Six

THE INSPECTOR

"Inspector, what do you think of all of this?"

"Well, I have watched people come and go from this resort; mostly women. I would see men go in, but never see them leave. I always thought there was something fishy about the place. I am glad it is gone. There was something sinister about it."

The officers comb the property and have not found any surviving tenants or staff.

"We have found nothing, Inspector."

"Oh, I don't doubt that. There won't be any remains of corpses."

"What do you mean by that statement, Inspector?"

"I just don't think we will find any remains."

"Inspector, my name is Chief Chase. Would you please come with me up the hill over there? I see something that may be of interest to you."

"What the hell do I see? It appears there are several mounds here, just like a burial site," says the Inspector.

"Yes, you are correct. The Coroner has already found many buried corpses, and they are all males."

"Hmm, that is why men would come but not go. What the hell

happened, and who the hell was the people overseeing this place?" questions the Inspector.

"Come over here, Inspector! What do you make of this one?"

"It is another burial site, but with a burnt corpse straddling it? It smells as if it was burned a few hours ago."

"The Coroner is almost certain the burned corpse is that of a female."

"And I will bet that the body under that mound is a male. Looks like some kind of a sad love story," says the Inspector.

"You may have something, Inspector. But, why only one burnt corpse on only one of the many graves here and she sure as hell didn't climb up this hill on fire?"

"That, I am afraid we will never be able to answer. Something sinister would be my guess."

IT IS FINISHED

- There will be no offspring.

- The resort is destroyed.

- The witches are dead, burned in the fire.

- The curse is removed.

"I Love You, Louie!"

"I Love You, Amanda!"

ABOUT THE AUTHOR

James Roberts, an emerging author of fictional Crime Thrillers, delivers to his readers the realization of twisted feelings, minds, and actions as well as true-to-life situations leading to criminal activities that are sometimes hard to fathom.

This book is James Robert's fifth.